I SPY & COLOR PRINCESS ☆ BOOK ☆

A
IS FOR
ARMOR

B IS FOR

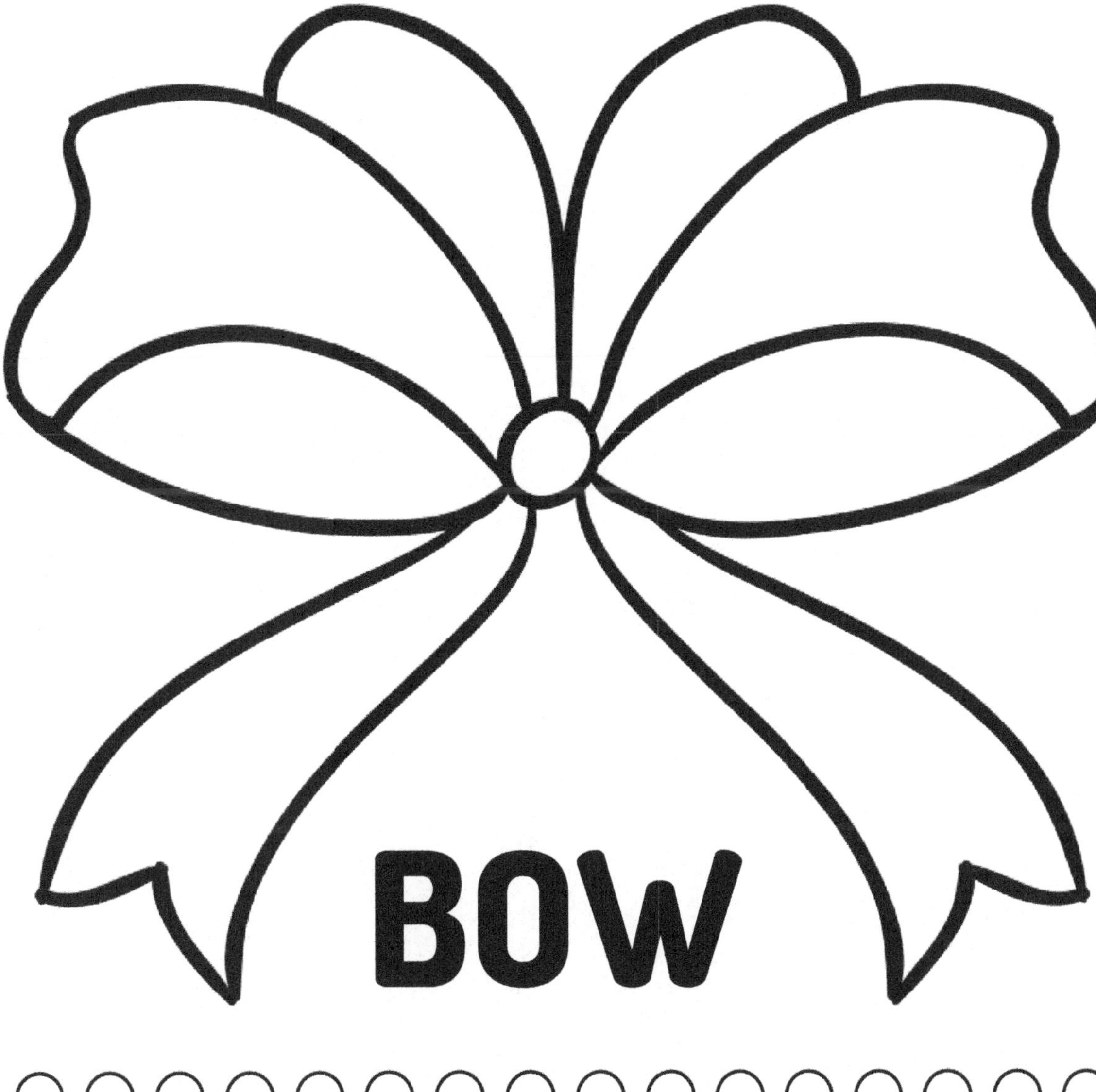

BOW

I SPY WITH MY LITTLE EYE SOMETHING BEGINNING WITH

D IS FOR **DIAMOND**

I SPY WITH MY LITTLE EYE SOMETHING BEGINNING WITH

E

E IS FOR

EARRINGS

I SPY WITH MY LITTLE EYE SOMETHING BEGINNING WITH

F IS FOR FAIRY

I SPY WITH MY LITTLE EYE SOMETHING BEGINNING WITH

G IS FOR GOWN

I SPY WITH MY LITTLE EYE SOMETHING BEGINNING WITH

I SPY WITH MY LITTLE EYE SOMETHING BEGINNING WITH

I

IS FOR

ICE CREAM

I SPY WITH MY LITTLE EYE SOMETHING BEGINNING WITH

J IS FOR JEWELS

I SPY WITH MY LITTLE EYE SOMETHING BEGINNING WITH

K

IS FOR

KING

I SPY WITH MY LITTLE EYE SOMETHING BEGINNING WITH

L
IS FOR
LIPSTICK

M
IS FOR
MIRROR

I SPY WITH MY LITTLE EYE SOMETHING BEGINNING WITH

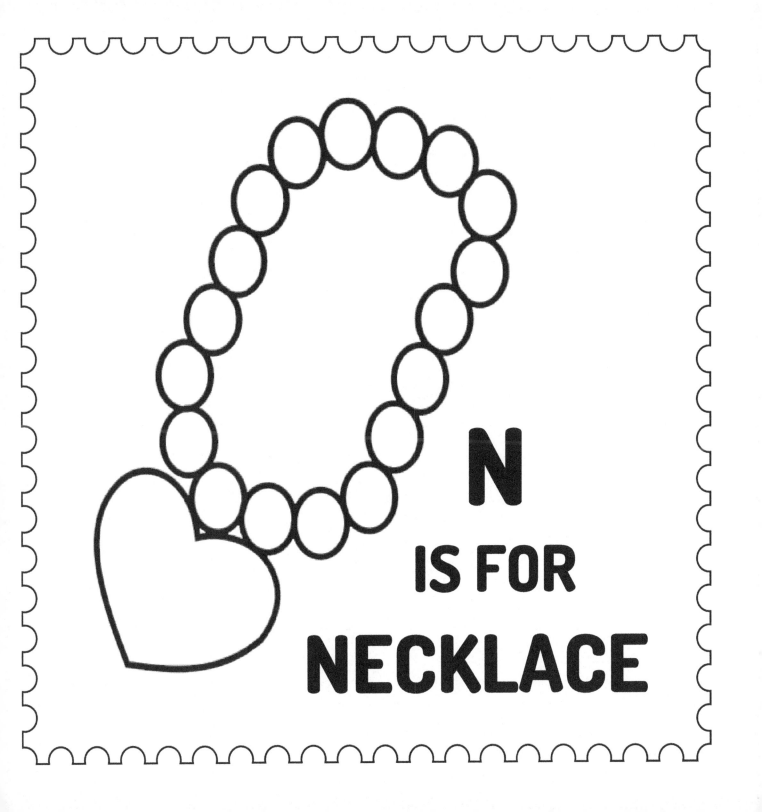

N
IS FOR
NECKLACE

I SPY WITH MY LITTLE EYE SOMETHING BEGINNING WITH

O IS FOR
ORNAMENT

I SPY WITH MY LITTLE EYE SOMETHING BEGINNING WITH

P
IS FOR
PRINCESS

I SPY WITH MY LITTLE EYE SOMETHING BEGINNING WITH

Q

IS FOR

QUEEN

I SPY WITH MY LITTLE EYE SOMETHING BEGINNING WITH

R IS FOR
RAINBOW

I SPY WITH MY LITTLE EYE SOMETHING BEGINNING WITH

S
IS FOR SLIPPERS

T IS FOR TIARA

I SPY WITH MY LITTLE EYE SOMETHING BEGINNING WITH

I SPY WITH MY LITTLE EYE SOMETHING BEGINNING WITH

I SPY WITH MY LITTLE EYE SOMETHING BEGINNING WITH

W

Royal Ball

W

IS FOR

WAND

I SPY WITH MY LITTLE EYE SOMETHING ENDING WITH

I SPY WITH MY LITTLE EYE SOMETHING BEGINNING WITH

Y IS FOR YARN

I SPY WITH MY LITTLE EYE SOMETHING BEGINNING WITH

Z
IS FOR
ZINNIA